Food Field Trips

Let's Explore Bread!

Jill Colella

Lerner Publications ◆ Minneapolis

Hello Friends,

Everybody eats, even from birth. This is why learning about food is important. Making the right choices about what to eat begins with knowing more about food. Food literacy helps us be curious about food and adventurous about what we eat. In short, it helps us discover how delicious the world of food can be.

I think that one of the most wonderful smells in the whole world is oven-baked bread. I love to eat fresh bread at dinner. My favorite way to eat bread is toasted with a bit of butter and cinnamon sugar.

For more inspiration, ideas, and recipes, visit www.teachkidstocook.com.

Jill

About the Author
Happy cook, reformed picky eater, and longtime classroom teacher Jill Colella founded both *Ingredient* and *Butternut*, award-winning children's magazines that promote food literacy.

Copyright © 2020 by Lerner Publishing Group, Inc.

All rights reserved. International copyright secured. No part of this book may be reproduced, stored in a retrieval system, or transmitted in any form or by any means—electronic, mechanical, photocopying, recording, or otherwise—without the prior written permission of Lerner Publishing Group, Inc., except for the inclusion of brief quotations in an acknowledged review.

Lerner Publications Company
An imprint of Lerner Publishing Group, Inc.
241 First Avenue North
Minneapolis, MN 55401 USA

For reading levels and more information, look up this title at www.lernerbooks.com.

Main body text set in Mikado. Typeface provided by HVD.

Library of Congress Cataloging-in-Publication Data

Names: Colella, Jill, author.
Title: Let's explore bread! / by Jill Colella.
Description: Minneapolis : Lerner Publications, [2020] | Series: Food field trips | Includes bibliographical references and index. | Audience: Age 4–8. | Audience: K to Grade 3.
Identifiers: LCCN 2019011161 (print) | LCCN 2019016647 (ebook) | ISBN 9781541581777 (eb pdf) | ISBN 9781541562998 (lb : alk. paper)
Subjects: LCSH: Bread—Juvenile literature. | LCGFT: Cookbooks.
Classification: LCC TX769 (ebook) | LCC TX769 .C555 2020 (print) | DDC 641.81/5—dc23

LC record available at https://lccn.loc.gov/2019011161

Manufactured in the United States of America
1-46461-47538-6/3/2019

SCAN FOR BONUS CONTENT!

Table of Contents

All about Bread 4
Let's Compare 7
Let's Explore. 9
Let's Bake Bread 11

Let's Cook. 20
Let's Make 22
Let's Read. 24
Index 24

Picture Glossary

ALL ABOUT BREAD

People all around the world eat bread. Bread comes in different shapes, sizes, and colors.

There are many ways to enjoy bread. You can eat it plain or with toppings. You can toast it or use it to make sandwiches.

French toast and croutons are made from bread. Bread crumbs make a coating for chicken nuggets.

LET'S COMPARE

There are many kinds of bread. Pita bread has a pocket inside. A baguette is long and crusty. Rye bread is darker than most other breads.

Naan is flat and round. Sourdough is crusty like a baguette, but it tastes sour! Can you count how many kinds of bread you've tasted?

LET'S EXPLORE

What is yeast? Yeast is a living thing! Can you see the bubbles? These bubbles become the holes you see in bread.

Yeast makes dough rise. It makes bread soft and fluffy!

YEAST IN ACTION

MATERIALS
- balloon
- dry yeast
- 1 tablespoon sugar
- ¼ cup (60 ml) warm water
- liquid measuring cup
- empty 16-ounce (0.5 L) bottle

1. Stretch the balloon by blowing it up and letting the air out.

2. Mix the yeast, sugar, and water in the liquid measuring cup.

3. Pour the mixture into the bottle. Put the balloon over the bottle's neck.

4. Leave the bottle in a warm place for 30 minutes and see what happens!

What might happen if you added more sugar?

LET'S BAKE BREAD

First, gather the ingredients. We need flour, water, yeast, salt, and oil.

Flour becomes dough when mixed with water. Water binds the ingredients together.

Yeast makes the dough rise. Salt adds flavor to the bread.

Mix the ingredients with a spoon.
The mix has turned into dough.
It is ready for kneading.

Kneading is pressing and rolling dough with your hands.

Why would we use a spoon and not our hands?

Stop kneading when the dough feels smooth. Pat the dough into a ball, and coat it with a bit of oil.

Place the dough into a bowl and cover it. When the dough is light and puffy, it is ready for the next step!

The dough grew! Now shape it into a circle.

Does the dough look different now? How?

Put the circle of dough on a baking sheet. Into the oven it goes!

Why do you think we say *bake bread* instead of *cook bread*?

Let's check the bread! When the crust is dry and golden, it is ready. Have an adult help you take it out of the oven.

Don't you love the smell of freshly baked bread?

LET'S COOK

Always remember to have an adult present when working in the kitchen!

BEGINNER'S BREAD RECIPE

The recipe serves 20. Share with friends or freeze it after it is made to make it last longer.

INGREDIENTS

- 1 packet (7 g) dry yeast
- 3 tablespoons sugar
- 1½ cups (360 ml) warm water
- 6 tablespoons (85 g) butter (3 softened, 3 melted)
- 2 teaspoons salt
- 4 cups (560 g) all-purpose flour (plus extra for kneading)
- 1 teaspoon vegetable oil
- oven mitts

1. Mix the yeast, sugar, and water in a bowl.

2. Add the softened butter, salt, and 2 cups of the flour. Mix. Add in 2 more cups of the flour. Continue mixing until you have a soft dough.

3. Lightly dust a flat surface with flour. Knead the dough for 6 to 8 minutes.

4. Rub oil in a clean bowl before placing the dough inside. Cover the bowl with plastic wrap. Place the bowl in a warm area for an hour or until it doubles in size.

5. Preheat your oven to 400°F (204°C).

6. Shape the dough into a ball, and divide into four even pieces. Shape each piece into a round loaf.

7. Let the loaves rise for 15 minutes.

8. Brush the loaves with melted butter.

9. Bake for 17 to 20 minutes, or until golden brown.

SEE THIS RECIPE IN ACTION!

LET'S MAKE

Use the bread dough from the recipe on pages 20–21 (steps 1 to 4) to make bread loaves shaped like bears.

BREAD BEARS

MATERIALS

- bread dough
- 3 tablespoons (42.5 g) melted butter
- oven mitt
- cooling rack
- raisins or chocolate chips (optional)

1. Divide the dough into 8 equal pieces.

2. Shape 4 pieces of dough into ovals for the bears' bodies.

3. Split each of the remaining dough pieces into 3 small pieces and 1 larger piece. It's time to build your bears!

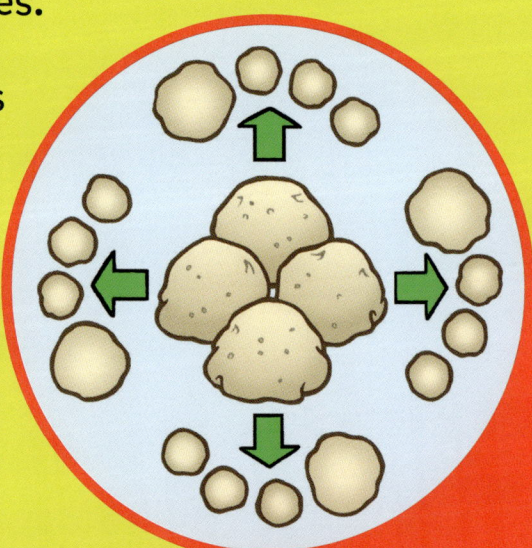

4. Shape the bigger pieces into balls for the bears' heads, and attach them to the bodies.

5. Take four smaller pieces and make two ears and one snout for each bear. Attach the pieces to the bear heads.

6. Split the remaining pieces in half. Roll each piece to create the arms and legs of each bear and attach.

7. Brush your bears with the melted butter, and let them rest for 15 minutes.

8. While your bears are resting, preheat the oven to 400°F (204°C).

9. When your oven is done preheating, it's time to bake your bears. Bake for 17 to 20 minutes, or until golden brown.

10. When your bears are ready, take them out using an oven mitt. Place them on a cooling rack, and let them cool down.

11. Optional: Make small holes where the eyes and nose should be and insert raisins or chocolate chips.

Let's Read

Bake for Good
https://www.kingarthurflour.com/bakeforgood/kids/

Binczewski, Kim, and Bethany Econopouly. *Bread Lab!* Seattle: Readers to Eaters, 2018.

Bread World
http://www.breadworld.com/

Heos, Bridget. *From Wheat to Bread.* Mankato, MN: Amicus, 2018.

Ridley, Sarah. *Seeds to Bread.* New York: Crabtree, 2018.

Index

baguette, 7–8

bake, 11, 17, 19, 21, 23

flour, 11–12, 20–21

knead, 13–14, 21

naan, 8

pita, 7

rye, 7

sourdough, 8

yeast, 9–12, 20

Photo Acknowledgments

Image credits: Moving Moment/Shutterstock.com, p. 1; Brent Hofacker/Shutterstock.com, pp. 3 (yeast), 6 (top); M. Unal Ozmen/Shutterstock.com, p. 3 (flour); Catalin Petolea/Shutterstock.com, p. 3 (knead), 15 (bottom left); La corneja artesana/Shutterstock.com, p. 3 (dough); SteveDF/iStock/Getty Images, p. 3 (bake); dbimages/Alamy Stock Photo, p. 4; Klaus Vedfelt/DigitalVision/Getty Images, p. 5 (top); Africa Studio/Shutterstock.com, p. 5 (bottom left); Floortje/iStock/Getty Images, p. 5 (bottom right); Beth D. Yeaw/Moment/Getty Images, p. 6 (bottom left); Joe Gough/Shutterstock.com, p. 6 (bottom right); Nitr/Shutterstock.com, p. 7 (top); wideonet/Shutterstock.com, p. 7 (middle right); Vlasovalana/Shutterstock.com, p. 7 (bottom); Sompote SaeLee/iStock/Getty Images, p. 8 (top); Kremena Ruseva/Shutterstock.com, p. 8 (middle right); 3445128471/Shutterstock.com, p. 8 (bottom); AngieYeoh/Shutterstock.com, p. 9; Tyler Olson/Shutterstock.com, p. 10; wavebreakmedia/Shutterstock.com, p. 11; RapidEye/iStock/Getty Images, pp. 12, 15 (bottom right); RichVintage/E+/Getty Images, p. 13; LightField Studios/Shutterstock.com, p. 14; successo images/Shutterstock.com, p. 15 (top); ffolas/Shutterstock.com, p. 16 (left); Warut Chinsai/Shutterstock.com, p. 16 (right); Pixel-Shot/Shutterstock.com, p. 17; Dean Mitchell/iStock/Getty Images, p. 18; Eric Audras/ONOKY/Getty Images, p. 19 (left); ClarkandCompany/iStock/Getty Images, p. 19 (right); fotostorm/E+/Getty Images, p. 20; Laura Westlund/Independent Picture Service, pp. 21, 22, 23 (illustrations); ZikG/Shutterstock.com, p. 22.

Cover: Plattform/Getty Images (family); Stephanie Frey/Shutterstock.com (sandwich); The Picture Pantry/Alloy/Getty Images (hands holding bread); Cinematographer/Shutterstock.com (close-up kneading dough).

Children's 641.815 COL
Colella, Jill,
Let's explore bread! /

AUG 2020